Chapter one

The car edged slowly off the highway into the gravel lot, leaving little trails of dust hanging in the air. A tractor trailer whooshed past, its tires whining on the hot pavement. Frank and I were leaning against the service counter, sipping cokes and talking about the merits of different cars we had owned or would like to own.

Looking between the stacks of tires

standing in front of the windows, we saw an old man get out of the car that had just pulled up. This was the first customer in over two hours at the tire store where we worked. We had already swept the floors clean, restocked the wheel weights and valve stems, sorted the used tires, and emptied the trash. Now we leaned against the counter with the front door propped open, enjoying a cool drink and some conversation. A small fan on the desk behind us oscillated the warm air about the room.

The old man opened the back door of his vintage Chevrolet, fished around on the seat and pulled out a small, dirty tire. He shut the car door, wiped the sweat from his face with his shirt sleeve, and walked toward the store.

"It's about time we had some business," Frank said. And he gulped down the rest of

his cola. It had been a slow day all along.
It was one of those clear hot days when the
farmers in southern Michigan want to get all
their field work done while the weather holds.
For the city folks, it was too hot to even go
outside unless they had to.

The old man ambled though the open doorway
and up to the counter. "Afternoon boys," he
said, as he placed the little ragged garden
tractor tire on the counter top.

"What can we do you out of?" asked Frank
with his best "Howdy neighbor" grin.

"Well," said the old man, "I've got to
have a tire like this one here, only without
all the holes in it, and with a little more
tread." He winked at us, thinking he had come
up with a pretty good joke. Too bad every
other guy who came through the door used it
too.

Frank and I gave him a polite laugh and I

examined the tire for the size markings. It
was an old tire for sure. The numbers read
400x6, 6ply. It had a ground driven tread,
much like a standard tractor tire.

"We have that size," I told him, "but not
that tread style, and it comes only in a four
ply." I said that maybe we could find
something like it in the tire book and order
it for him.

"That'd be alright. I won't be needing
the tractor for awhile," he replied.

Frank thumbed through the rack of tire
books at the end of the counter. He found the
one on farm and implement tires and plopped it
down in front of us. Flipping through the
pages, he looked for the correct size and
tread type. Skipping the tractor rears, he
stopped at the planter tires, scratched his
chin with his thumb as he thought, and went on
to the wagon tires. On the facing page was a

section on tires to fit lawn mowers and garden tractors.

"That looks like it," the old man pointed at one. He was leaning over the counter, trying to read the book upside down.

"Looks good, but comes in the wrong size," Frank said.

After looking through the book, we discovered that we couldn't even order the tire that the old man needed. The brand name on this tire had been scuffed up from years of use so we couldn't even tell what it was. Frank suggested a couple dealers in town that he thought might be able to order the tire.

"I'm not surprised you don't have it," the man said. "This tire's twenty years old at least," and he pointed at the tire laying on the counter, all dry and rotted, with traces of dirt still stuck between the worn out cleats. "It came on the garden tractor when I

bought it. That was, oh,... ten or twelve
years before I retired. My back isn't too good
so I got out a few years early," he explained.
He smiled and looked around the store at all
the stacks of tires as though he'd run out of
things to talk about and was looking for
ideas. I hadn't met a retiree yet that didn't
have enough to talk about.

"What model garden tractor do you have," I
finally asked.

"Old Ford," he replied.

Well, I knew there had to be about 50,000
old Ford tractors still running around the
country, taking just about every size tire
that was ever made. There was everything from
lawn mowers to farm tractors. Most people
seem to forget that you don't know exactly
what size their car, truck, or as in this
case, garden tractor, takes, even though
you've never seen it. After a polite pause, I

asked him the year and model of his old Ford tractor.

"Don't rightly know about the garden tractor," he replied. "But my big tractor is a Ford 8N," he said proudly. "About a '50. Best darn little tractor ever made too!" His face beamed, and I could tell that he was off and running. A light shone in his eyes as he gripped his garden tractor tire in his large gnarled hands and said, "It runs just as good as my old Model A." As though there were any doubts in our minds.

"Oh?" Frank said slowly. "You've got a model A Ford?" And he leaned further over the counter. Both of us were old car buffs and Frank's dream was to own a Model A.

The old man sensed our excitement. He had us hooked now. The conversation was his. He said that seeing as how he didn't have much to do that afternoon, and he wasn't in much of a hurry and all that, he'd tell us about his car.

"Runs like a top," he said. "I'll go to my grave in that car if my wife'll let me."

Frank's excitement faded a little. I knew he was thinking that the old man had at least ten or twenty years left. Frank wanted an "A" before that.

"Yep," continued the old man, "Best car I ever had, and I've been driving for well over fifty years now. Got my license back in thirty-four. You only had to be fourteen back then. Not so many cars on the road either. Back then my grandfather owned a combination gas station and coal yard. Now, my dad and Uncle William worked the place for Granddad, as he was getting up in years and he also tended to drink a bit. Drank more'n his share, ya might say, and left running the business to dad and Uncle William.

Well," the old man continued, "Granddad owned a Model A Ford like the one I have at home... no,..." He paused and thought a bit. "It was a Model T. It had wood-spoke wheels and wasn't quite as nice as the newer Model A. My Model A has a clutch, brake and gas pedal. The Model T had a low and high forward pedal, a reverse pedal and the brake pedal. The parking break and clutch release lever were to the driver's left. The gas was on the steering wheel."

Chapter 2

"Anyway, one Friday night Granddad got drunk, as usual, and on the way home he ran off the road and hung the car up on a cement abutment at the edge of town. The car was balanced so that no matter what he did, it'd just sit there and teeter back and forth. The back wheels would touch for a second, just long enough to throw some gravel, and it would teeter back to the front again.

The next morning I was hanging around the station with my two cousins, Jim and his little brother Archie. Archie was just a little cuss, being only eight years old at the time. So while we were bothering dad and Uncle Bill, Arch was bothering us. He'd follow us everywhere. Well, Granddad came walking up the sidewalk, what sidewalks we had were wood, and he asked us if we wanted his old Model T. Naturally he meant Arch too. But we didn't care too much, seeing as how we didn't have a car anyway. He told us what the situation was, but that didn't dull our determination one bit. No sir! We set out with jacks and blocks and we worked the rest of the morning getting that thing off the wall. How he ever got that car up there, we could never figure out.

Well, we got it off and drove it back into the middle of town just as proud as can be. I was the driver, seeing as how I was only one with a driver's license. My cousins didn't mind, 'cause they were just tickled to death to have a real car. Arch was so glad to be along with us that he actually kept his mouth shut and sat back in the rear seat real proud and stuck out his chest like a banti rooster. He felt like one of the big guys. We waved at our friends all the way through town 'til we got to the coal yard.

I pulled the car up to the pumps and we jumped out and ran inside to tell our dads about grandpa giving us the Model T. Funny thing about dad and Uncle William; they just winked and smiled at each other when we told them the news and said, "That's nice boys," in a funny kind of way like they knew something we didn't.

They gave us a gallon of gas for helping out that morning and we decided we'd do us some fishing. Now I have to tell you about

our new gas pumps. We sure were proud of

them. Dad and Uncle William had replaced the

old pumps, where we had to crank the gas up to

a clear container and let it drain down, with

new Bennett clock face pumps. The company was

right here in Michigan too. Well, after

getting our gear together, we drove out to our

favorite fishing hole. Our cane poles were

tied to the roof of the Model T, the twine

tied off on the front and rear axles. The car

had no bumpers.

Once we were in the country I let Jim

drive the rest of the way, seeing as how he

was just dying to get behind the wheel. He

had to let Arch steer some too, just to keep

the little snot happy.

Jim pulled the Model T to a stop 'neath a

big shade tree and I jumped out and got my

fish pole ready. Jim just sat behind the wheel

for a minute, staring at the gages and
pretending he was in the Indy 500. I had to
'pert near drag both of 'em out of that darn
car. Then they wouldn't come down to the
creek, just walked around it and touched it
here and there.

I spotted a great big paper wasp nest
hanging from a branch right over our car. I
started talking to Jim, and while I did, I
stuck the tip of my fishing pole into the
nest. I told them that if they weren't going
fishin' then I'd go by myself, and I pulled
the tip of my pole out of that wasp nest and
headed down the trail. I didn't get more than
two rods away when I heard Jim let out a yell.

"Sweet Jesus," he bellowed, "Hornets!,
Hornets!"

I could hear Archie's little voice
screeching and his little feet running around
the car. He didn't even threaten to tell on

Jim for using the Lord's name in vain. Well, the commotion went on for about ten to fifteen seconds when down the trail they came. Jim was running like to save his soul from Hell itself, and Arch was right on his heels, his little legs just a blur.

"Help Jimmy, help," he yelled, and they went by me doing what seemed to be just over a hundred and ten miles per hour.

They disappeared behind the brush and I heard them hit the water with one big splash. I went down to help them out of the creek. They'd lost those hornets a long way back.

Jim hadn't been stung but once, and that was on the hand where he'd tried to brush one off. Arch was a different story though. His right ear had swelled up like a cauliflower and he was bawlin' his head off. I even started to feel sorry for him. We went plodding back up the trail to the car, Jim and

Archie's sodden clothes squishing and dripping with every step. They were the sorriest looking fellas I'd seen in a long time.

"I never knew that nest was there," said Jim, sucking on the side of his hand.

"M...M... Me neither," stammered Arch, in between sobs.

"I can't figure out what could have gotten into them," I said. "They just seemed to go crazy all at once. You guys didn't do anything to stir them up did you?" Both swore that they hadn't.

Back at the car, the wasps had thinned out some. They were still buzzing all over the nest and a few strays would come by every minute or so, but we could still get in the car and head for home. I drove as fast as the roads would allow, as Archie's ear was looking pretty bad. He sat in the back sobbing and holding his hand to the side of his head.

We got Arch home and his mom fixed up a poultice for his sore ear and sent him to bed. Jim wrapped his hand in a wet rag containing baking soda and we drove on down to the gas station to tell our dads. It was almost six o'clock, time for closing. They usually closed up the coal yard at four and then someone hung around the gas station until six.

We pulled up out front and parked. My dad was repairing a tire and Uncle William was pumping gas into a brand new '34 Chevrolet. It was the dentist's car. He drove nothing but a Chevy, said you couldn't beat 'em. When he drove off, Uncle William said he figured that he owned just as much of that car as the dentist did, what with all the time his family spent in the chair and all.

Granddad was sitting up on the gas station porch, playing checkers with Smiley Potter. Smiley Potter was the town bum. Every town

had one, and Potter was ours. I never knew
his first name. Everybody just called him
Smiley. He was an old cuss. He'd been old
ever since I could remember. And he tended to
be on the heavy side. I didn't ever know
where he lived. About the only time I ever
saw him, he was sitting on the gas station
porch. Or, in the winter, inside by the pot
bellied stove, playing checkers and telling
stories. He always had a chew of tobacco in
his mouth and he'd spit into an old coffee can
he carried with him. It seems there was
always a stream of tobacco juice running down
his chin from one side of his mouth. It'd get
so far and just when I thought it would drip
onto his grubby shirt, he would wipe it off
with the back of his hand, which in turn he
wiped on his pants. He never had a job that I
knew of. My mom, Aunt Alice, and Grandma
didn't approve of him at all. But Grandpa

seemed to like him well enough, even though he was the most no account I'd ever met.

Well, Granddad and Smiley were playing checkers when we drove up. Granddad asked if he could borrow the car for an hour or so as he and Smiley "Had a few errands to run." Granddad had me fill up the gas tank of the Model T for him. "I don't know what I'd do without you boys," he said with a broad smile as he and Smiley climbed in and drove off.

As they pulled out the drive, I heard Smiley scream and cuss out a blue streak a mile long. I never knew cuss words could be used in such wonderful combinations. It seems one of those wasps had crawled out from the crack in the seat and stung him right on his broad rear end. And Granddad didn't bring the car back. We figured it was gone forever.

Chapter 3

Two weeks later it was the middle of June
and it was hot. Down at the gas station,
cousin Jim and I sat on the edge of the porch
sipping on orange Nehis bought from the
machine just inside the door. Jim had a big
black beetle bug crawling back and forth
between his feet. He had a stick that he'd
poke it with when it got close to his foot,
then it'd turn around and head the other way,

leaving little tracks in the dust. This was all the energy we could come up with to entertain ourselves. We wanted to go swimming, but both of us were too hot to walk out to the swimming hole. Archie was busy listening to Smiley Potter tell another one of his lies about fighting the Kaiser over in Europe during the Great War.

About this time Granddad came up the street, sweating up a storm. He walked up to where we were sitting and glanced at our soda pop and said, "Hot day, ain't it, boys. It's enough to dry a man right out, what from having to walk two miles into town and all."

Smiley Potter said to Archie, "Jump up from that chair boy, and let your poor grandpa sit down." Old Smiley knew which side his bread was buttered on.

Granddad collapsed into the chair. "Darn car gave up the ghost," he said in an irritated voice.

"Huh?" said Archie.

"Conked out. Quit. Died just outside of town. Had to walk two blamed miles in this hot sun. Sure am thirsty," replied Granddad, starting to sound a little pathetic now.

Smiley patted his pocket as if he might have had a nickel stuck in the seam or something, then said, "Darn it, Chester, I'd buy you a soda, but I spent all my money already," and he nodded toward us like he was the one who bought us our Nehis instead of ourselves. Smiley never had an extra nickel that didn't go for liquor or tobacco.

Cousin Jim and I just looked at each other. We knew that one of us was going to have to break down and buy the old goat a pop. Archie didn't have any money either. He never had any. Being the wealthiest of us boys at the moment, I volunteered. I didn't even know

Granddad liked soda pop. He asked for grape.
Probably reminded him of wine.

"I don't know what I'd do without you
boys," Granddad said with a big smile as I
handed him a bottle of grape Nehi.

"That's right!" chimed in Smiley.

Granddad sat on the porch slurping at his
bottle of pop and smacking his lips. "That
car's got a busted freeze-out plug," he
finally said. He held up a rusted round piece
of metal a little bigger than a quarter.

"Back in those days," said the old man,
"We used alcohol in the radiators of cars so
they wouldn't freeze up. They didn't have
permanent anti-freeze, and alcohol tended to
boil out if you didn't watch it." The old man
paused to collect his thoughts.

Frank and I nodded, intently following his
story so far.

"Anyway," the old man continued his story,

"Granddad had a freeze-out plug in his engine block pop out that spring when it got cold again one night and froze. He just tapped it back in with a ball peen hammer and refilled the radiator with water. It always leaked some after that and finally gave out on him that hot day. He said he guessed he'd sell the old car for junk, which was for about five or ten dollars. He seemed to have forgotten that he'd given the car to us several weeks earlier."

Frank and I shook our heads in disbelief. Ten dollars for a Model T Ford! We leaned closer over the counter. The old man looked at us both, enjoying our complete attention. He cleared his throat, then he went on.

"Well, we asked Granddad if we couldn't have that old car. He said he guessed so, seeing as how it wasn't any good anyways. So he gave it to the three of us again.

Jim and I went to buy a new freeze-out plug for the engine block, but found out that the garage didn't stock that size anymore. They'd have to order a plug from a warehouse. We didn't want to wait, so we bought one the next size larger. Then, while we were walking the two miles out to get the car, Jim and I took turns filing the large one down to the size of the defective original that Granddad had dug out of a pocket of his bib overalls and given to us. He'd found it in the dirt under the car. We had to be real careful to keep it round. After one gentle file, I'd turn the plug a tad, then take another gentle swipe. We walked in the hot sun out to the car and finally got that plug filed down so's it'd fit. After cousin Jim tapped it into place with the ball peen hammer we'd brought, along with a cider jug full of water, we drove the car to the first house and topped off the radiator from the hand pump out in the yard.

Well now, we drove into town just as proud as could be in that car. We yelled and waved at all our friends. I drove straight to the gas station and bought two gallons of gas. Dad said we were lucky Granddad hadn't warped the engine block or the cylinder head.

We had decided to go swimming. Cousin Jim and I got to leave Archie behind this time as our dads didn't want us forgetting about him and letting him drown. We left the poor kid behind to watch Granddad and Smiley Potter play checkers in the shade of the gas station front porch.

Pulling up to the swimming hole, we saw three bicycles lying on the ground. They belonged to three girls that Jim and I went to school with. Two of them were sisters. Mary was seventeen and her little sister Margie was fourteen. The other girl's name was Sally, and she was about fifteen or sixteen at the time. Now, we couldn't figure out what they were doing there, for as far as we knew, that was our secret swimming hole.

There was a place back toward town where most of the kids went swimming, but a few of us had our secret places where we could skinny dip in hot weather and not be bothered.

We snuck down the trail to the creek. The water made a slow bend there and was about thirty to forty feet wide, and not over four feet deep at its deepest. We came to some bushes along the bank and there were all three girls' clothes hanging on the bushes so as not to get dirty. We could hear the girls laughing and splashing out in the water.

"Holy cow," Jim whispered, "This is gonna be better'n the ladies underwear section of a Montgomery-Wards catalog!"

Being best friends as well as cousins, we

both knew each others' experiences and adventures. Neither of us had ever had a chance at anything like this. Jim parted the bushes real careful like, and we peeked out, both as nervous as chickens in a fox den.

The sun was shining toward us, and it glared off the water. The girls were sitting or kneeling on the river bottom so that the water was up around their necks. We really couldn't see a dog-gone thing! Jim just stood there in front of me, bent over low, peering through the parted bushes, staring real hard. I was peeking over his shoulder. Neither of us moved. Then Sally stood up and I about fell over backward. Man, that gal was built like a brick outhouse! Jim tried to swallow and all he made was a sort of funny gurgle sound like he was chokin'. Sally always had a reputation for being well built. Well, here was proof right before our very eyes. My

throat went suddenly dry, and I thought my
heart was going to stop.

Finally we got tired of watching and ran
up to the river bank.

"Hi girls," we yelled. "Water warm?" and
we pulled off our shirts like we were going to
strip and jump right in. There was such a
screaming and a carrying on, you'd a thought a
mad 'coon had broken into the hen house. The
girls dunked under water clear up to their
chins and threatened to tell our moms if we
didn't leave.

Jim grabbed a dress and held it up in
front of him and paraded around.

"Put our clothes down," the girls yelled.
"We'll tell your dads if you don't," they
threatened.

"Come on out and take them," Jim shook the
dress he was holding up just a little harder.
He always was a quick thinker.

"You'd like that, wouldn't you," one of the girls yelled.

No one accepted the challenge though, so after a few more minutes of our teasing and their threatening, we tossed their dresses onto the bushes and walked back to the car. Jim drove about a half mile down the road to another spot he knew of. He parked the car in a grassy trail and we hung our clothes on a tree limb and jumped in the river. The cool water sure felt great after the heat of the day. The current seemed to wash our tiredness right on down the stream. There was a tree that had pulled loose its roots and fallen into the water. Jim showed me how to dive into a shallow hole on the down-stream side of the trunk. Man, that was living!

I was sitting in the water watching Jim get ready to try a flip from the tree trunk, when we heard a voice.

"Yoo hoo! Boys."

We both looked around. Those three girls were standing on the bank holding our clothes. I yelled and Jim turned beet red and leaped into the water with a big splash. "Put our clothes back!" we shouted.

"If you want them, come and get them," they chanted in unison, giving us a taste of our own medicine. They held our pants and my shirt up to their waists and danced around. Jim looked at me and I knew what he was thinking. We both charged for the shore splashing fountains of water ahead of us. The girls stood there a moment, shocked. Then they began screeching, and throwing our clothes down, ran back up the path. We chased them all the way to the road, naked as jaybirds. Jim was leading up the trail, stepping lightly with his bare feet, and Sally would stop once in a while and stare back at him, her eyes as big as saucers. The girls jumped on their bicycles and pedaled off to town faster'n a hound with his tail on fire. They hadn't planned on us coming out of the water at all.

Later, after a long discussion about girls, and those three in general, I drove the car back into town and pulled up at Uncle William's house. Marsha and Sally came riding by just as Uncle William asked how the swimming was.

"Okay, I guess," Jim answered his dad. "What can you do in the water?" The girls let out a chorus of giggles and stopped their bikes by the car. They wanted us to go bicycle riding with them. We had a better idea, and offered them a ride in the Model T. Archie wanted to go too, but thankfully Uncle William made him stay put.

That night Jim borrowed a dollar off me to

take Sally to the movies and for an ice cream afterward. And I'll be darned but five years later they didn't up and get married."

"That just goes to show you," interrupted Frank, "That you never can tell."

"Yup," replied the old man, "and they still live in the old home town. He runs the coal yard now. Added a lumber yard too, and had four kids to boot."

"By the way," he said. "You got a pop machine around here? I'm feeling a little dry myself," and he dug into his pockets for change. I pointed to the machine that stood against the wall. It was so close that it would've squashed him flat if it'd fallen over just then. He patted his pockets some more and smiled kind of sheepishly like his change must have fallen out through a hole or something.

Finally, Frank couldn't stand it anymore. "Here's a quarter," he said. "It's on the house."

The old man clinked the coin in the slot,
studied the buttons for a long moment, like he
thought he'd get a shock if he pushed the
wrong one, then made his selection. He opened
the bottle and took a big gulp and sighed.
"Hits the spot. I thank you boys."

I couldn't help but notice he'd selected
grape, and I had a feeling we'd just been
conned.

"Well," he went on, "The next day was
Sunday. Granddad came by the house and woke
me up to ask if he could borrow the car to
take Grandma to church.

"Go ahead," I told him. "I won't be
needing it this morning."

As he left I heard him tell my dad, "I
don't know what I'd do without those boys."

With a clearer head I sat up and looked at
my clock. It was ten o'clock. Grandma had

been in church for an hour. She usually
walked over to the Methodist Church with my ma
and little sister. They always sat in a pew
with Aunt Alice.

If Granddad was going to church, which I
thought unlikely, the second coming must have
been scheduled for that night.

Around noon my cousin Jim came over. He'd
promised Sally a ride in the car. He even was
willing to let me drive so he could sit in the
back with her. Well, he pert near had a fit
when he found out that Granddad had borrowed
the car again. He said we'd never see it now
'til a month after Christmas. To help calm him
down, I walked over to Sally's house with him.
We wouldn't be caught dead on our bicycles now
that we'd owned a car. We explained why there
was no car. Sally didn't seem to mind a bit,
but did invite us into the house for some of
the best apple pie I ever ate.

Chapter 4

Another Saturday morning rolled around and cousin Jim and I were working for our fathers down at the gas station, trying to make an extra nickel or so. I was sweeping up the floors and the porch while Jim was out back emptying the trash barrels. We'd been arguing over who had to clean the bathrooms and that task still lay ahead of us. I could do the gents room alright, but I sure didn't want to be seen cleaning the ladies room. I was bent over, picking up some gum wrappers when I heard Granddad driving the Model T up Main Street. Something was wrong. I could tell from the sound of the engine. Standing up, I watched him steer the car into the lot. Dad and Uncle William came around the corner of the station from where they'd been changing the oil and lubing the police chief's Hudson.

"Why, he's finally blown a head gasket," Uncle William said.

"Sure has," Dad replied. "We tried to warn him about that, didn't we?"

"That we did," Uncle William agreed as he shook his head slowly while turning to go finish the job on the Hudson.

"I'll take care of him," Dad said as Granddad stopped the car in front of the gas pumps. A cloud of steam forced its way out from under the chassis and through the cracks

of the hood. Granddad got out of the car and
slammed the door, making a loud, tinny,
rattling noise. Smiley Potter popped open the
passenger door and nearly tumbled out into the
dust before catching himself on the door
frame. They'd been drinking already, again.

"I'll never own another Ford," Granddad
grumbled. "This thing is nothing but trouble.
Rather have a horse," and he left the car
sitting forlornly at the gas pumps in a small
cloud of vapor. He walked unsteadily up the
three wooden steps and onto the porch where I
was standing. He flopped heavily into one of
the wooden chairs perched there in the shade.
Smiley Potter followed behind, taking the
other chair.

"Sure could use a drink," Granddad said.

"Looks like you've had a few already," Dad
told him from the ground.

"Hmmpff," said Granddad. "You boys sure

are smart mouthed towards your old pappy," he complained. "Now, what you gonna do about that old car?" he demanded, while pointing unsteadily at the still steaming Model T.

"Guess we could junk it out. Or maybe give it to the boys here," Dad answered.

"Well, then I won't have a car," Granddad grumbled. "Course, that old thing isn't much of a car now, is it?" He rubbed his whiskery chin while he thought about it. Smiley Potter slumped in his chair, looking like he was fast asleep. Or maybe dead. I couldn't tell which.

Dad looked up at me. "Well son, guess you boys have a car again," and he turned and disappeared around the corner of the station to where the Hudson rested over the outdoor grease pit.

I leaned my broom inside the door, by the pop machine, and hurried down the steps and around the corner. Dad was just coming from a shed out back, carrying something in his hand. It was a head gasket for a Model T Ford. He grinned broadly while holding it out. Cousin Jim had just put a trash barrel back in its place and was hustling over to see what was up.

"Let that thing cool down, then install this," dad said while handing me the gasket.

"Be sure to get the torque wrench," came Uncle William's voice from under the Hudson. "It'll work without it, but heck, why take a chance?" he added as he was climbing up the concrete steps of the grease pit. Wiping his hands on a rag, he continued, "We'll give you boys a hand if you need it, but it's not hard at all."

That afternoon, with Dad and Uncle William leaning on the Model T while Jim and I changed the head gasket, we learned a little more about auto mechanics, and a little more about our fathers. They really didn't help us much, mainly kept an eye on us and shared stories about how *they* learned auto mechanics, and about all the times they had to bail out their father when he took to drinking. It's a wonder Granddad ever was able to start and keep a business running. It turned out that Dad and Uncle William had a lot to do with it, even though they were just teen-agers.

The next day cousin Jim and I were at Jim's house making plans to take the Model T and go fishing. Archie wasn't home for once, and we were in a hurry to get our gear around and beat it out the door before he got back. Aunt Alice had prepared a couple of meat loaf sandwiches for us to take for a later snack. They sat, wrapped in old newspaper, on the kitchen counter. Just then little Archie came tearing across the side yard and up across the front porch, calling for us to come out. He burst into the front room as we turned to see what all the racket was about. With Arch, no one could be sure if it were a real emergency or not. Aunt Alice hurried in from the kitchen, wiping her hands on her floral apron, her face etched with worry. Archie paused to catch his breath.

"Fred McDonald caught a giant snapping turtle," he finally blurted.

Cousin Jim and I looked at each other doubtfully.

"What on earth?!" Aunt Alice exclaimed.

"A turtle," Arch repeated, sucking in more air. "Come quick! He can't last much longer! It's on the old logging trail behind his house, by the mill pond! It's huge!" Archie exclaimed with a wave of his arms. Little Archie was easily excited, but this topped anything I'd seen before.

"Yea, right," Jim replied sarcastically.

"You boys had better go," Aunt Alice

urged. She was still wiping her hands on her apron and eying Archie sympathetically.

"Mommm," Jim begged.

"Come on!" Arch insisted. "It's the biggest turtle I've ever seen."

"James Robert," Aunt Alice said firmly.

"Let's go," Jim admitted defeat. "Get in the car, Arch. We'll drive down."

Archie beat us out the door and down the steps and across the yard to the Model T and climbed in.

"Hurry!" he yelled out the window. Jim and I trotted down the porch steps and over to the car. I slid behind the wheel and Jim climbed up on the passenger seat and slammed the door. I mashed down on the self starter and adjusted the spark on the fly. Pushing on the reverse pedal, the car groaned and rattled, and we backed out the driveway. Within moments we were heading down the street

to the south edge of town where the McDonald
house sat between two large vacant lots that
used to be horse pastures, and now served as a
base-ball or football field for the
neighborhood kids.

"Faster. Go faster!" Archie urged from the
back seat.

"You want to get there alive?" Jim called
over his shoulder. "We're going thirty miles
per hour as it is. Jeez! Darn little kids."
Jim was irritated about missing his fishing
trip.

"You said darn," Archie reminded him.

The driveway that led to the back of the
McDonald property came into view. I slowed
and took the corner as fast as I dared.

"It's back there," Arch pointed ahead out
the windshield. "He's halfway up the pond
hill, on the trail."

"How did he catch this supposedly giant

turtle?" Jim asked. I couldn't help but
notice his voice was dripping with sarcasm.
Archie didn't pay any attention.

"Is it really a snapper?" I inquired.

"Yea, the biggest I've ever seen. He
grabbed it on the millpond bank. We were
trying to catch bullfrogs for frog legs. Fred
grabbed it by the tail and it nearly pulled
him in. He couldn't let go or it would get
away. We couldn't pick it up by the tail
because it's too heavy. It stuck its neck way
out and hissed and tried to bite us. I didn't
want it to bite my finger off, so I wouldn't
touch it and I told Fred I'd go get help.
He's probably had to let go by now." Archie's
words came tumbling out, almost too fast to
understand.

We jounced back the narrow lane, the long
grass and Queen Ann's lace brushing the side
and the bottom of the car. Topping a low rise

I braked to begin the sharp decent that I knew
lay on the other side.

I knew of the McDonald kid. He was about
Archie's age and we'd seen him around the
lakes and rivers fishing and swimming with the
other guys. He was a typical little kid, but
wiry and wasn't afraid to tackle a challenge.
I couldn't see him grabbing a hold of a giant
snapper though. They could be mean.
Downright vicious if need be. Even the older
guys treated them with respect and tended to
give them a wide berth. However, turtle soup
was a rare treat that Mom or Aunt Alice
prepared whenever someone donated a snapping
turtle to the cause.

We crested the rise and I could see the
curly red hair of Fred McDonald about halfway
up the hill. He had a hold of something with
both hands and was slightly bent over, bracing
his bare feet into the sandy gravel of the

47

trail. He looked up expectantly when he heard the rattling and commotion of the car, his sweat streaked, freckled face tight with concentration.

Archie had his head hanging out the car window like a dog going for a ride. All he needed was a long tongue to hang out and let flap in the breeze.

"Hang on! We're coming!" he bellowed to his friend.

Pulling to the side of the lane, I hit the brake and stopped the car. Shutting off the engine, I left it in gear and cranked the wheels sharply to the right to keep the car from rolling down the hill, and maybe even rolling over one of us. Archie was already trying to squeeze out between the front seat and the door frame. Jim flung open the door and Arch popped through, hitting the ground running. Jim and I hurried to catch up. I could tell that Fred had caught hold of something big. As we approached I saw just how big it was. His little hands had a white knuckle grip on the tail of a huge moss-backed snapping turtle. Leaches were attached here and there to its legs and body. It was trying to claw itself free from Fred's grasp. The monstrous neck was stretched out and arched back while the mouth hung open ready to latch on to anything put in its way. Jim snatched up a big stick and stuck it where the mouth could snap shut on it.

"I've got it," I said to Fred. He let go with a little sigh of relief, rubbing his cramped hands. I quickly tightened my grip on the turtle's tail.

The huge snapper had left claw marks in the dirt where Fred had dragged it from the pond. There were patterns in the dust where he stopped to rest and the turtle had continued to struggle.

"I'm sure glad to see you," Fred said to us. "I couldn't hold it much longer. That turtle is really strong."

"And heavy too," I added, lifting it by its tail. Jim hoisted the front end by the stick that was still clenched in the turtle's mouth. Between the two of us we walked the turtle to the car. I looked over at Arch who was walking beside us with Fred and watching our every move. "You were right, Arch," I told him. "This thing is huge."

"Biggest I've ever seen," Jim emphasized the "I've" as he nodded his head at Archie, who was beaming from ear to ear. Fred ran along ahead to pull open the driver side car door that stood ajar from when we hurried out.

"On three," Jim said, "One, two, three!" and he and I swung the turtle up and onto the floor in the back. It promptly let go of the stick and hissed and snapped at us. We'd made it mad.

We stepped back and I slammed the door. Circling the car a few times, we clambered onto the running boards to peek in through the windows, all the while trying to draw up the courage to climb in and drive back up the lane to Fred's house. Finally the turtle calmed down and quit moving around. I cautiously opened the driver's door and gingerly climbed in, half afraid that the turtle would come charging over the seat at me. Jim opened the passenger side door to allow Arch and Fred to scamper onto the back seat and crowd together on the passenger side. They eyed the snapping turtle, still on the floor behind the driver's seat, and kept their legs and feet pulled up on the seat, well out of range.

"Why can't we sit in front with you guys?" Arch wanted to know, a tinge of worry in his voice.

"He won't hurt you," Jim called over his shoulder. "Don't be a sissy. How you doing back there, Fred?" he queried.

"Great so far," Fred replied. "As long as that turtle stays on his side, that is."

Jim and I looked at each other and grinned. I straightened the wheels and let the car coast a few feet before mashing down on the forward pedal. The engine coughed to life and I drove down the trail to get a running start to back up the trail. The hill was so steep I didn't think the Model T could drive up it forward. All of the gas would slosh to the back of the tank, which was mounted under the front seat. Being gravity flow, the gas supply couldn't reach the engine from the back of the tank, so I decided to use the old Model T owners' trick and back up the hill.

We made it to the top of the hill just fine. I backed off the road and pushed on the forward pedal. Away we went up the trail, jouncing along while Archie and Fred tried to avoid the angry snapper on the floor in the back.

Following Fred's instructions, I pulled the car up near the old horse barn, now converted to a garage. Shutting down the car, Jim and I climbed out, allowing Fred and Archie to beat a hasty retreat from the back seat.

"Let's put it in this old wash tub," Fred said while running to the side of the barn and retrieving a galvanized tub. He dragged it by one handle, rattling and thumping across the yard. He dropped the tub by the driver's side door and peered through the side window.

"How we going to get it out of there?" I asked Jim.

"I was hoping you'd have an idea," he said. "Because I haven't a clue."

Fred disappeared then came out of the barn with a flat scoop shovel and a rake. "Open the door," he happily called. "I'll get it out." He positioned himself by the door and I turned the handle and stepped back. I half expected the turtle to come charging out at us. Nothing happened. I peered around the door. The turtle sat hunkered down on the rubber floor mat, it's beady little eyes watching us maliciously. Fred steadily moved the rake into the back and over the turtle. It stuck its head out and up and hissed violently. I had to admit, for a little kid, that Fred had nerves of steel. He didn't flinch. Next, he slid the shovel across the floor of the car toward the turtle, which made a jab at the leading edge. The shovel stayed put. Fred pulled the rake up against the turtle's shell and scooted the shovel underneath it.

"I can't lift it," he said to us as he strained at the end of the handle.

I grabbed the shovel handle as Fred stepped aside. Using his foot, Jim pushed the wash tub closer to the running board as I slid the turtle out. It was heavy and I had to choke up on the handle, fearful that I might get too close. I got it into the wash tub more or less gently. Fred and Archie danced around with excitement. Jim and I shook our heads and grinned.

"What are you going to do with it now?" I asked.

"Make soup," Fred answered. "And look at this over here." He motioned for us to follow as he and Archie hustled around the corner of the old weathered barn. We rounded the corner to see him and Arch pointing at the barn wall.

There, nailed to the old gray boards, were a half dozen large turtle shells, but none larger than the one currently scratching around in the wash tub.

After leaving the McDonald's house, we drove down to the coal yard to tell our fathers about the giant turtle we'd helped Fred McDonald catch. Granddad and Smiley Potter were playing checkers, using the top of an old wooden barrel as a table for the checker board. They looked up as we pulled into the coal yard. Jim and I leaped out of the Model T and hustled over to tell them about the turtle and how large it was.

Granddad stood up. "I've got to see this thing," he said. "Course I'll need to borrow the car from you boys. Can't walk down there in this heat ya' know."

"I'll come with you," Smiley stammered as he slid back his chair and stumbled to his feet. The two of them climbed into the car.

Smiley was yapping about turtle soup and

Granddad said something about getting a drink.

He hit the wrong pedal and the car lurched

into reverse. Jamming on the forward pedal,

Granddad made the Model T change course, and

down the street they went. The car was gone

from our lives again.

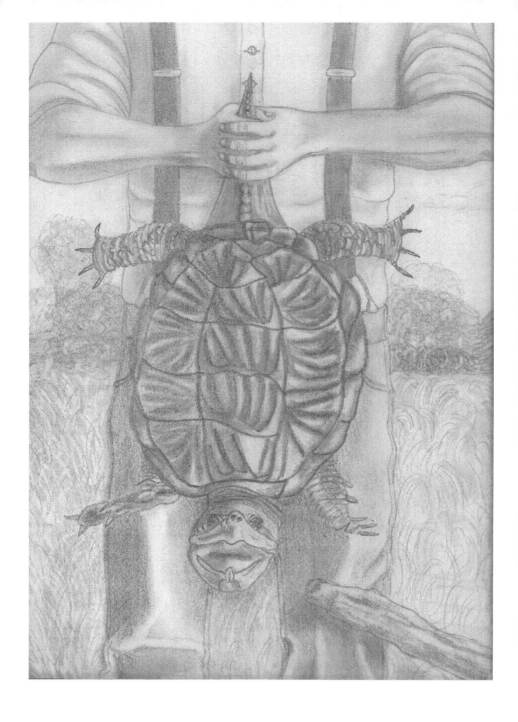

58

Chapter 5

    Well now, the Fourth of July came and we'd

all but forgotten about that car. There was a

big parade scheduled for down Main Street at

ten A.M. Afterward, everybody would go over to

the school grounds for all the games and

square dancing. There was baseball, a greased

pig contest, and tug-o-war, just to name a

few. We used to get pretty excited about the

Fourth back then.

About nine o'clock, Jim and I were down at the coal yard helping out, trying to earn some extra spending money and getting ready to watch the parade go by. We were located just a block away from the spot where the parade started. Next thing you know, Granddad came limping in with the Model T. The right front tire was flatter'n a dog what'd been run over by a Packard. It was flopping and smacking on the concrete as he eased off the road.

Smiley Potter was with him so we figured that they'd been doing a little drinking already. We were right. They sort of sloshed out of the car.

"Whatsa' matter, Smiley, ya got troubles?" Jim asked.

"Does the bear live in the woods, boy? Course we got troubles. That tire's flatter'n a wet rag," and he pointed unsteadily at the flat tire, like we hadn't noticed.

Jim and I exchanged grins.

It was getting fairly warm out already, and Smiley was sweating like a plow horse. He puffed his way up the porch stairs, sounding like a steam engine climbing a long hill, and collapsed into a chair. "Good enough place as any to watch a parade," he said.

Granddad looked at the car and shook his head real slow. There wasn't a spare tire.

"We haven't any tires in stock for that," Dad told him.

Granddad said he just might as well trade it in on a different car. He just about had enough of it. It was nothing but trouble. Then he saw Jim and me standing there and said, "Course, if you boys want that old thing then I guess you can have it."

But what good was a car with only three tires?

Granddad said he needed a drink and down

the street he tottered. Smiley stumbled to his feet and followed along. I turned around and saw my dad wearing a big grin. He motioned for us to follow him around back of the gas station. There, leaning up against the back wall, was a tire to fit our car. It was mounted on a Ford wheel and ready to go.

"The thing's been laying around here for a year now," he said. "Just might as well use it."

We rolled the tire around front and put it on the car while the parade went by. Then I started up the T, Jim jumped in, we waved good-by to our dads, and followed the parade through town. All the kids on decorated bicycles were riding around the car and we waved at everyone we knew. Sally and her family sat on a blanket at the edge of the street. Jim wanted her to ride with us so I stopped the car and she ran out and climbed in. Jim winked at me, then climbed in the back to sit with her.

After the parade I parked the old car at the school yard and we walked around for a while. Dad and Uncle William had entered the team horseshoe pitching contest. They had both always been pretty good and were on their way to defeating the defending champs. Jim and I cheered them on for awhile and then had to leave as we were entered in the pie eating contest. But even with Sally cheering us on, we lost. Later we tried the sack race and came in second. Can't remember what the prize was now, but we were proud as peacocks. That is until little Archie came running up with a duck tucked under each arm. He'd won the ducks by tossing canning jar rings over their heads while they swam around in a horse trough.

Jim and I had tried that game earlier. We

didn't think there was any way possible to get those little rings around those fat ducks' necks. The ducks had one leg tied to a string that led to a weight at the bottom of the horse tank. There was no escaping that way. Those ducks in the tank were half scared out of their wits. They were dodging and darting about. It was near impossible to hit one, let alone ring it. But here was Arch, all excited and the ducks a flapping and quacking up a storm.

He wanted us to help take them home. He was going to shut them in the basement and then come back and win some more. People were looking at him in amazement. Some stopped to admire his prizes which were still braying and flapping at the air, struggling to free themselves from Archie's ever tightening grip. It started to take on the appearance of a riot. Little downy feathers were floating in the air and pin feathers littered the ground.

One little boy tugged at his dad's shirt, pointed at Arch, and cried. "I want a duck like that kid's, Dad!"

His dad dragged him off saying, "We'll see son, we'll see."

Well, we didn't want to leave and miss any of the action. Jim has always been a good speller and was entered in the spelling bee, which was going to start pretty soon.

About this time Granddad and Smiley Potter came walking up. They'd been over at the beer tent most of the morning. Granddad saw Archie's ducks and said something about how nice they'd be for Sunday dinner. This set Archie to howling. And the ducks, which had calmed down some, started back up a flappin' and a carrying on again. Smiley was babbling like an idiot, and wiping his face on a dirty handkerchief. By now he had about as much sense as sheep in a stampede. Finally Granddad told him to shut up. Then he offered to take Arch and his ducks home, if he could use the car, of course. Jim and I said "Fine."

Granddad said that he had a small errand to run anyway, and he didn't know what he'd do without us boys. He made a big deal about how he was right proud of the way we fixed that tire up. The old goat was too snockered to know it had to be a different tire. They shuffled off amidst the ducks' commotion and that old fool Smiley babbling about duck stew.

Jim won a stuffed dog for coming in first in the spelling bee. He gave it to Sally. And Granddad didn't bring back the car. I didn't think we'd ever see that Model T again."

The old man paused again for effect and to gather his thoughts.

Frank and I looked at each other in disbelief. Finally I said, "Go on."

66

Chapter 6

The old man collected his thoughts again.
Frank and I glanced at each other as we waited
for his next story.

"I sat bolt up in bed," he began.
"Somewhere off in the haze of my sleep I had
heard sirens. Our phone rang; three longs,
three shorts, three longs again. There was a
fire. I leaped from bed and hurriedly
dressed. I was still hopping down the

hallway, attempting to put on my shoes and tie them between hops. Dad's voice came from downstairs. He was talking on the phone. Not everyone had a phone back then. Especially during the depression, but Dad and Uncle William had to have one as they were on the fire department and they ran a business. The dining room light was on. I heard the click of the porch light switch and Dad's voice say to Mom, "The school-house is on fire. I'll be a while, I'm afraid."

"Be careful," Mom's voice sounded worried.

I finished tying one shoe and paused at the top of the stairs.

The sound of an engine pulling up out front let me know that my uncle's '32 Ford pickup had arrived. I heard Dad as he went out the door, closing it softly behind him.

The town's fire chief had retired and died in 1929. There was no official chief now.

Dad and William were the most experienced and everybody got along with them, so running the show was pushed onto them.

I made it to the bottom of the stairs without breaking my neck.

"You boys be careful out there. And stay out of the way." Darn. Mom had read my mind.

Footsteps on the porch let me know that cousin Jim had arrived. Uncle William had let him off when Dad had gone out. Then he and Dad had sped away with a whining coming from the old Ford's transmission and the click of the gears being shifted.

"Bye Mom," I called as I met Jim on the porch. I blew her a kiss as the heavy oak door latched behind me.

"Let's go," Jim said hurriedly. "Dad says the whole school is going up."

We started down the street. The school was several blocks away, on the other side of our small town, just off Main Street. We could see the shimmering glow reflecting off the clouds in the night sky. It was hard to believe that only a few weeks before, the populace had celebrated the Fourth of July on the grounds surrounding the building.

As we turned onto the street leading past the school, it seemed the whole town had turned out. Everyone but Mom at least. Crowds lined the sidewalk on either side of the fire equipment. Smoke drifted to us and I could hear the flames crackling and popping. From a distance we could see that the town tanker truck and pumper were on the scene with trucks from two other departments. We walked down the middle of the street toward the fire. Behind us a siren kicked in. Jim and I jumped to one side as spectators cleared the street. A tanker truck from yet another town was coming toward us, headed to the fire. Three firemen were packed in the cab with four others in a four door Ford following closely behind. Uncle William and another man, whom I didn't know, came down the street from the direction of the flames, clearing the crowd out of the way. Jim and I jumped in front of the tanker truck and led the way, waving our arms and shouting "Fire truck coming through. Clear the street please." Uncle William saw us and stopped where he was until we reached him.

"Thanks boys," he said. The man with him smiled and nodded our way. They both looked tired and smelled of smoke. We turned and walked four abreast down the middle of the street back toward the fire. The tanker truck, an old converted REO, ground into low gear and crawled along behind. At the fire scene, Dad and two other men ran to the street carrying a heavy leather hose. The tanker creaked to a stop and the firemen poured from the cab. One worked quickly to ready a valve to attach the hose. The engine revved to a high idle and the men ran off with the hose nozzle to reinforce the other departments.

The new firemen from the car behind the tanker came running up. "What can we do," one of them, who I took to be the chief, called out to Uncle William.

"I've got some barricades coming," William replied. "When the truck gets here, block off the street. We've got to keep the crowd out of the way if we can." He had to almost yell to be heard over the crackling and popping of the burning school, the roar of the pumper engines, and the shouting of the firemen as they coordinated their attack on the flames.

Jim pulled his watch from his pocket and checked the time. "2:55," he said. "We'll probably be here 'til daylight."

I nodded in agreement. In my excitement I'd never bothered to check the time at home. The call must have come through from the switchboard about 2:00 o'clock, I reckoned.

About this time the flatbed truck from the village showed up with some wooden barricades piled on the back. The men from the other department unloaded a few and Jim and I helped set them up across the sidewalk and around the trucks in the street. The men followed the flatbed to the end of the street and set barricades up there too.

They had just finished blocking the street when my granddad's model T turned the corner that Jim and I had just walked around twenty minutes prior. To get around the barricade, he had to jump the curb. I could see the right front wheel turn out at an odd angle as he came up the street. Something was bent out of whack from hitting the curbing. Granddad had his head out the window yelling at people to get out of his way. He waved his arm for effect. Fortunately, most people had already left the street so he could wobble the old Model T on up to the fire engines.

"What now?" Uncle William muttered to himself. Granddad got out of the car. I could tell he'd been drinking.

"Oh boy," Jim said to me from out the side of his mouth.

Granddad walked on over, albeit a little unsteadily, and surveyed the scene. He shook his head. "It's a gonner," he said. "Best you can do now is containment." He stepped closer, taking in the whole picture and the bustling activity. Hoses snaked across the lawn in front and around the school. Men hustled and shouted. Sprays of water shot into the roaring conflagration, and mist filled the air.

As if on cue, the roof collapsed amid a
shower of sparks and debris shooting skyward.
The firemen backed away as one body. The
crowd went "Ooooo," and took a step back too.

"Let 'er burn," Granddad remarked with a
wave of his hand. "Just hose down the
neighbors' roofs." And he walked away. I was
impressed that the old guy knew that much
about fighting a fire. In front of the T,
Granddad stopped, as though transfixed. "Look
at that," he finally exclaimed. "Bent a tie
rod." Then he muttered to no one in
particular, "This old car is going to be the
death of me yet," and he started walking away
from the scene, down the street toward Main
Street. He only stumbled a few times,
apparently being used to intoxicated walks
about town in the middle of the night.

"What about your car?" Uncle William
called after him.

"Give it to the boys," he grumbled in reply. He didn't look back. Just waved a hand over his shoulder and kept walking.

Uncle William watched him go and shook his head slowly before turning his attention back to the fire.

"Good thing he didn't get close enough to the flames to breathe on them," Jim said. "They'd have felt the explosion clean over to Albion."

I laughed in agreement.

Within a couple of hours, the flames had died down. Jim and I helped the men from the other departments roll up a few hoses and tidy up the street. They'd been pouring water onto the flaming hulk of our old school all night. Now there were just some glowing embers and smoldering piles of beams in what was the basement. Even from our safe distance, Jim's and my eyes smarted from the smoke and our

clothes were slightly damp from all the
moisture in the air. Most of the crowd had
cleared out for home by now. Only a few die-
hards remained, ignoring the barricades and
talking to the firemen as they rolled up hoses
and secured equipment. Some ladies from the
Methodist church arrived with sandwiches and
coffee and lemonade. Uncle William's Ford
pickup was parked across the street and the
ladies got busy distributing the refreshments
from the tailgate. Grateful firefighters
dragged themselves over in groups of twos and
threes to fuel up.

A newspaper reporter showed up a little
after five A.M. He roamed around getting in
the way of the firefighters and talking to
Uncle William. He spoke to a few of the
chiefs from the other towns before taking some
pictures of what was left of the school. He
took a few more of the fire equipment to wrap

up his story. Before he left, he asked Jim
and me where the best place was to get
breakfast.

"At my house," Jim replied, then corrected
himself. "The Downtown Cafe' opens at six.
Tell them the chief's son sent you," he added
with a grin. Jim looked at me, hoping I
caught the joke, seeing as how his dad really
wasn't the fire chief.

"I'll do that," the reported called as he
climbed into his new Terraplane and started
the motor.

The eastern sky was turning slightly pale
when Dad came over with Uncle William. "You
boys better go get some sleep," He said. His
own eyes looked bloodshot and tired. His face
appeared more haggard than I'd ever seen it
and his voice was raspy from shouting and
inhaling smoke. Uncle William didn't look
much better.

"You know," Uncle William said, "When we were kids, my dream come true was to have the school burn down. Now that it's happened, I realize just how much the town has lost. Our heart and soul is in this school. I know we'll rebuild, bigger and better too, but, boy this sure takes the wind out of a man's sails."

My dad clapped his hand on his brother's back. "I feel the same, Bill," he replied. Then eying the Model T, he looked at us boys.

"Think you two can get that car down to the station sometime today?" he asked. "We'll have to get a tie rod from Western Auto or the Ford garage if we can't straighten it."

With that he turned and walked to the town pumper engine, opened the door, and fished around under the seat. Withdrawing a four pound sledge hammer he walked back over to the Model T. Laying on the pavement, he crawled

half-way under the car and swung the sledge a
couple of times, loudly banging on the bent
tie rod. The turned out tire straightened a
little. Satisfied, dad crawled out, stood up
while brushing off some dirt, and walked over
to put the hammer away.

Cousin Jim and I tiredly climbed into the
Model T. Jim on the passenger side, I behind
the wheel. I mashed down on the self started
and the engine fired up. Uncle William
slapped the top of the roof twice, and waved
us on. Dad winked his eye and jerked his hand
up in a tired wave. I didn't know if he
winked on purpose or because his eyes were
still burning from all the smoke.

I dropped Jim off at home and headed to my
own place where I left the T in the driveway
and headed off to bed. Mom caught me in the
hallway, took one look and whiff of me, and
marched me into the new bathroom Dad and Uncle

William had installed a year ago. She left me
with instructions to shower off.

"You'll not be getting onto clean sheets
in this house all covered in soot and smelling
like a bonfire," she said.

I hadn't realized that I looked that bad.

"Wait 'til you get a look at Dad," I
countered. Somehow I made it through a shower
rinse and crawled into bed. The hall clock
chimed six-fifteen. As I drifted off to
sleep, I wondered if the reporter was enjoying
his breakfast at the Downtown Cafe'.

I awoke later and, opening my tired eyes,
looked at the clock. Eleven thirty in the
morning. Almost noon. Even drunks like
Granddad didn't sleep this late. I swung my
feet out of bed and onto the floor, trying to
remember all that had happened last night. My
brain was still foggy from the late hours and
disruption of my sleep routine. Walking to

the window, I pulled back the curtain that mom had thoughtfully closed, and peered down to the yard below. The Model T was still in the driveway. I hadn't dreamed that part after all.

The house was silent. The door to my parent's room was closed. Walking downstairs and into the kitchen, I discovered Mom preparing lunch for herself.

"Oh, you're up," was her response when I entered. She smiled brightly. "You boys must have had quite a time of it last night," she said. "Father told me all about it when he came in. He and William are awfully proud of you two." She beamed at me again. I attempted to rub the grit from my eyes, blinked sleepily, and sat down at the table.

"When did he get in?" I croaked.

"Little past eight-thirty. William is going to put a closed sign in the station window for the morning. Dad figured you boys could pump gas 'til they got around." She slid a sandwich toward me and began to prepare another one. I became aware of the radio on the shelf faintly playing music by Benny Goodman as my mother hummed a little song to herself.

"Who's watching the fire?" I asked, somewhat clearer now. My throat ached a little.

"Some fellas from the other departments are going to keep an eye on it while our guys get some sleep," Mom replied. "It's too bad about our school," she added while placing a large glass of cold milk in front of me. "Doesn't seem all that long ago that I graduated from there."

"Hmm," I nodded.

Finished with the sandwich and milk, I said "Goodbye," to Mom and walked stiffly out to the T and started it up. My body ached all over. Now I knew what it was like to feel old. The T smelled faintly of wood smoke.

Mom promised to call Jim to tell him I was coming. He was standing at the street when I pulled up in front of his house. He looked tired as he opened the car door. I tried to act cheerful and refreshed. He looked at me through bleary eyes.

"You're not fooling me," he said. "You're tired too."

"Umm hmm," I responded. "Throat sore?"

"Yes."

"Let's go pump some gas," I replied, and we rode in silence down Main Street to the edge of town and the coal yard and gas station.

Granddad, of all people, was sitting up on the porch, tilting back in one of the chairs. He smiled broadly at us as we climbed out of the Model T.

"Well now boys," he greeted us. "Nice to see you survived your first big fire." He tilted the chair back down to all four legs and nodded approvingly. He seemed as fresh as a three year-old after a long nap. As it was a warm day, the door to the gas station stood open. The "closed" sign was nowhere in sight. "Glad you fellas showed up. I can stand to be spelled for a while. Promised to check on the boys watching the fire." He looked at his watch. "Almost one o'clock," he said. "You boys take over. I'll run on over to the school. That is, on over to what's left of the school," and he grinned broadly again. He stood up and motioned to me to take his seat. Jim plopped tiredly down in the other.

I sat down and closed my eyes. I heard Granddad's footsteps go down the wooden steps from the porch and the crunch of his shoes on

the gravel. I opened my eyes to the sound of
the Model T being started.

"Don't know what I'd do without you boys,"
he called as he put the car in gear and headed
down the street. I was sure we'd never see
the Model T again. Of all the times we'd had
the car, this was the shortest yet. Through
bleary eyes, Jim watched the T move away, the
right front tire still looking a little
awkward.

"Maybe he'll fix the tie rod before we get
it back," he mumbled, and his eyes fell shut.

Chapter 7

After the school burned down, the village fathers had a big meeting with the school board, which was half of the village fathers anyway, and tried to decide what to do about a school system. Here it was, the end of July and we had no school building. The town couldn't build one in a month and have it furnished by the end of Labor Day.

After much discussion, it was decided that

the high school would meet downtown in the old opera house. The elementary would hold classes above some of the store buildings. A few of us on the west edge of town would transfer to the Bath Mills School located about two miles out. It was a large one-room school that was considered very modern by nineteen thirties standards. Their student numbers were low, as most of the kids came into town for school, so about twelve of us switched over temporarily, until our village could erect a new building.

The country school was on the bank of a small creek that fed directly into the Kalamazoo river. In the eighteen hundreds there were a grist mill and several houses located there, along with a railroad station and livestock shipping yard. They all had burned or had been torn down by the early twentieth century. Only the school and a few nearby farm houses remained, testament to what once was a thriving village.

It was here that I would begin my tenth grade education. The whole idea sounded a lot better to me when cousin Jim talked it over with Uncle William and he was allowed to attend with me. We told Archie he had to stay in town with the other babies. He didn't seem to mind too much. The school boards met together and decided that when the new school was built, Bath Mills would consolidate with the town school. The old building would be used as a community hall and 4-H meeting place for the rural neighborhood. The two boards agreed to merge right away and my dad and Uncle William were volunteered to be on the board to coordinate with the country part. Dad was delighted that maybe we'd pick up some more farm boys for the football team, come next year, instead of having them drop out. This would be incentive for them to stay in school.

We started school in the fall, right after Labor Day. We town kids thought we were hot stuff, and soon dominated the school. There were only about ten or so country kids at this point. They went through the eighth grade and if they wanted to continue on, transferred into town, so this was a homecoming of sort for about five or six of our classmates. The younger kids sat in the front while we older kids sat in the very back. There was only one student in a higher grade, a girl in the eleventh. Three seniors, one fourth of the graduating class, got to stay in town with the senior class. Can't say as I blame them, their last year at school and all. This left us with twenty-four students in the school. Most of them elementary.

The building had clapboard siding which the neighbors had painted white. There was a main entrance with double doors. On the right side was what the teacher called the boys' cloak room and on the left the girls'. A small supply closet held chalk, paper, paint and such, and toilet paper for the outhouses located out back. One outhouse was for the girls, another for the boys. They sat about ten feet apart, with the doors facing the back of the school, and their back walls facing the little creek that flowed past about twenty yards away.

We were cautioned by the teacher and the country kids not to play in the creek during recess. If we fell in, we might get a whipping. To the west and the east and south was one large cornfield that stopped at the creek. The school was a little island in the sea of corn. We town kids were fascinated by the creek and by the corn fields. Several towering maple trees dotted the front

playground and the west yard. The east yard
and driveway were open.

The teacher was a young woman in her early
twenties. I don't recall her name now. She
wasn't a bad sort. But there were times when
we really ran her ragged and she'd get after
us. Especially us older kids. She had the
school organized so that we older students
read or studied while she worked with the
little kids. Then we started our lessons
which were written each day on the blackboard.
If we needed an explanation, she'd come to
help if another student couldn't. We older
kids assisted the lower grades too. I kinda
liked how it all worked out. We really knew
our stuff what with the studying and teaching
all mixed together.

There was an oil heater that sat in the
middle of the room for the cold weather
months. On a table behind it was a large,

brown, earthen-ware crock that held our
drinking water. A spout dispensed water into
a community cup that hung on a nail at the
side of the table. Usually the teacher or an
older girl filled a pail at the pump out
front, near the swing sets, and filled the
drinking crock.

Jim and I never volunteered for anything.
We did our work and, as soon as school was
over, headed out the door. We could walk to
school or ride our bikes, which we didn't want
to do. Most usually Dad or Uncle William
would give us a ride out and pick us up. We
always gave other kids rides if they needed
it. Their parents did the same. I don't
recall anyone having to walk unless it was a
nice day and they chose to.

A few weeks into the school year Uncle
William was taking Jim and me to school. Just
outside of town where the road turned to

gravel, we came upon an old car buried up to its right rear hub in the mud stirred up by a heavy rain the night before last. The driver must have gotten too close to the edge of the road to mire the car like that.

"I know that car!" Uncle William exclaimed. "You boys should too. It's yours!"

"It is!" I responded. I sat by the door and hung my head out the open window for a better look. Jim leaned forward to peer through the truck's dusty windshield.

His dad pulled the pickup to a stop up in front of the car and backed up while easing over slightly to get a little closer to it. "I wonder what the old goat's got himself into now," William asked no one in particular. "Hop out boys. There's a tow chain in the back. Hook it to the axle on the T and to the bumper on the truck. Then see if the key's in

the thing. If so, start it up and we'll pull
it out."

Jim and I followed his instructions. We
were in luck. Granddad had left the key in
the car. I flipped on the mag, adjusted the
spark and gas, and hit the self starter. The
engine turned over a few times then rattled to
life. Jim stepped up on the running board and
waved his dad on. Uncle William eased the
pickup into the chain. I pushed on the
forward pedal into low speed and took my foot
off the brake. The wheel spun in the mud.
The pickup started to throw gravel at us with
stones and mud splattering against the
windshield. As the mud released its grip on
the Model T, it slowly inched up onto the
level road. Uncle William stopped the truck.
I put the T into neutral while Jim raced out
and stepped on the tow chain to get us some
slack. Kneeling down in the gravel, he

reached under the axle and unhooked the chain. His dad had already unhooked the other end and he took the chain from Jim and tossed it into the back of the truck bed where it landed with a surprisingly loud metallic rattle.

"You boys got enough gas to get out to school and back?" he asked. I nodded yes. He climbed into the truck, slammed the door, and pulled into a gravel farm lane to turn around as Jim and I drove off to school.

The farm kids treated us like royalty when we showed up in that old Model T. We had to let them sit in it at recess until teacher came out and put an end to our fun. I couldn't help but notice that she looked it over with raised eyebrows and a grin on her face.

One warm day toward the end of September or maybe early October, Jim and I were out back exploring the corn field while the other kids played at recess out front. I noticed the corn silk was turning dark brown from its normal green. Teacher had told us that there's one thread of silk for each kernel of corn on the cob. That had us curious, so we had to go look for ourselves.

Jim pulled some silk loose. "I wonder," he said, "if this stuff will burn. It looks a lot like tobacco. Here," he said to me, "Take a look."

I took it and rubbed it between my index finger and thumb.

"Seems like I heard somewhere that people smoke this stuff," I replied. "If we only had something to roll it in."

"How about some toilet paper?" Jim asked. "There's a roll in the supply closet. I'll go get it," he said.

Students were expected to take the roll with them on visits to the outhouse and return it to the closet when through. I believe it

was teacher's way of keeping an eye on the

stock. I waited patiently at the edge of the

cornfield.

Jim soon returned with a roll of toilet

paper. We picked some silk. After several

tries, we had what faintly resembled a

cigarette.

"Let me try," Jim said.

I pulled a wooden kitchen match from my

pocket while Jim practiced puckering his lips

to hold the cigarette. I lit the match on my

zipper, and cupping my hands around the flame,

stuck it to the end of the cigarette Jim held

between his lips and the thumb and index

finger of his right hand. This was gonna be

great!

Jim puffed on the cigarette. The toilet

paper went poof! The corn silk fell to the

ground with a few glowing sparks. Jim looked

disappointed for a moment. Then we both
laughed at the joke we'd played on ourselves
as we stomped out the few embers on the
ground. Out front, the sound of the recess
bell sounded. Recess was over.

"What do we do with this toilet paper?"
Jim pointed at the roll I held in my left hand.

"The two of us can't walk in with it.
Teacher will know we're up to something," I
replied.

Jim thought a moment. "Gimme that and
follow me," he beckoned as he started walking
across the grass to the back of the girls'
outhouse, toilet paper now in his hand.

"What are you doing?" I asked, a little
confused.

"Just you see," he replied. He bent over
and unlatched the clean-out door that was at
ground level. A little eye hook held it up
out of the way. We could peer inside to the

dark recesses of the pit area of the outhouse.
Jim plopped down on the grass on his stomach
and began peeling off toilet tissue. "Here,
help me with this," he said, handing me a wad
he'd just ripped from the roll.

Following his lead, I shredded the paper
and tossed it into the opening. It took a
while, but working together, we finished the
roll.

"Gimme a match," Jim said.

I pushed into my pocket, and retrieving
one, handed it over. We lay on our stomachs
in the grass, talking quietly for a few
minutes when we heard footsteps on the gravel.

"I hope it's a girl," Jim whispered.

Moments later when we heard the door to
the girls' outhouse open, we knew we were in
luck. Jim's eyes brightened. He held the
match near his zipper. We waited a bit for
the occupant to get situated, then Jim lit the

match and tossed it in the pit on top of the shredded toilet paper. We were rewarded with a loud "whoosh" as the methane gas and toilet paper went up in the blink of an eye. It couldn't have gone better. We put our hands over our mouths so our victim wouldn't hear us snorting and snickering. Our bodies shook convulsively as we enjoyed our trick. The outhouse door squeaked open then slammed shut. We knew our terrified victim was heading back to school to tell teacher.

Our merriment was short lived however as the next moment someone's hands gripped our shoulders tightly and helped us to our feet. Rather roughly, I might add. Good grief, it was the teacher! We'd set the teacher's butt on fire!

"Here's where you two are!" she fairly shouted. "I wondered what became of you," she said.

Suddenly our joke wasn't funny anymore. Jim stared at the ground.

"Yes'm," he replied. I grunted in agreement.

"What if one of the little girls had been in there?" she demanded. "She could have been badly burned."

"Yes'm," Jim replied again. I couldn't even grunt in agreement as she forcefully assisted us around the corner and to the front of the school, still tightly gripping our shirts.

"For a little lady, she sure has a lot of strength," I thought.

"I'll be speaking to your fathers," she said through clenched teeth as she deposited us at our desks and marched to the front of the room. I'd never seen her angry before and she looked like she could take on the U.S. Army. The rest of the class stared at us wide-eyed. Nobody said a word.

The afternoon seemed to drag on. Finally dismissal came. The students filed out, giving us inquisitive looks as they walked past. Two girls lugged out the earthenware crock and dumped it to the side of the yard before setting it, empty, back on the table near the stove. The teacher was busy with the telephone that hung on the wall near her desk in one corner of the room. She hung up and turned to us.

"This isn't gonna be good," I whispered to Jim, who was trying his best to look contrite.

"Your fathers are on their way out," she stated calmly. "You boys are to remain here."

"Yes ma'am," we both replied, glancing at each other.

In what seemed within minutes, Dad pulled up out front. Granddad was with him. Uncle William's old Ford pickup soon followed, and

then two more cars belonging to other school
board members.

"Holy cow!" Jim whispered to me.

"We had really done it now," I thought.

The teacher called us up front and had us
sit on a couple of stools facing the rows of
desks. All we needed were some dunce hats.
Our fathers came in looking a little sheepish
themselves.

"Where's the key to the car?" Dad asked.
I dug in my pocket, the one that held the
matches, and handed it over. He in turn
handed it to Granddad who smiled broadly,
winked at us boys, then turned and left. I
could almost hear him say, "I don't know what
I'd do without your boys."

Dad and Uncle William greeted the two
other school board members by name, and all
four sat on the desks at the front row.

Teacher launched into the events from her

perspective. She had turned the class over to the oldest two girls and had gone into the yard to look for us boys. Nature had called and she made a visit to the outhouse when "the incident," as she called it, occurred.

When she had finished, Dad and Uncle William and the school board members looked at each other. I thought I could detect the slightest trace of a smile on the faces of the men. Maybe I wasn't going to die after all.

Dad cleared his throat. "What were you boys thinking?" he asked. He sounded rather exasperated. I was really sorry I'd disappointed him. He and Uncle William had trusted us to be responsible, he told us.

"Not only could the teacher have been injured, but you two have broken her trust too," he said. He was really laying it on thick. Uncle William hadn't even started yet.

About this time, we heard the Model T come

to life out in the drive. Granddad had finally gotten it started, or had paused long enough to sneak a quick drink before heading out.

"I guess I wasn't thinking," Jim answered.

He never mentioned trying to smoke corn silk. I was glad of that. Looking at Dad and Uncle William sitting there, I suddenly realized where I'd heard about people smoking corn silk. It was from Dad. He'd told Mom about it once while we were in the car driving to the house of one of his friends for a visit in the country. I had stood on the rear seat, leaning forward and clinging to the back of the front seat, hanging onto his every word. I remember my mom laughing over how dumb Dad and Uncle William were when they were kids. Now here Jim and I had done something dumb too. Only even worse.

It was now Uncle William's turn. I don't

recall what all was said, but he finished up by telling us that we owed the young lady, the teacher, an apology. We both looked at her.

"I'm sorry," I said. "I don't know what I was thinking and I'll try my best to earn your trust again." I thought that was pretty good for not having any time to practice.

"I wasn't thinking at all," Jim started. "I now realize how badly someone could have been injured. I can assure you that you'll not have to worry about outhouse tricks from me again." He managed a feeble smile. I noticed how his speech was better than mine. What a kiss-up. I also couldn't help but notice how the teacher's sour mood seemed to melt.

"Apology accepted, boys," she smiled sweetly.

Our fathers and the school board members seemed to relax and one of the members cleared his throat to speak.

"Thank goodness all is well," he said. "In the future this will not be a problem. When the consolidation is complete, the new school will have proper bathroom facilities." He chuckled to himself at his joke.

The others brightened up considerably. All except Jim and me. I could tell by Dad's glances that I wasn't off the hook yet.

The other board members shook Dad's and Uncle William's hands and left. Our fathers escorted us outside. Jim climbed into his dad's pickup and I slid onto the seat on the passenger side of the family Studebaker. The school teacher locked the double doors to the school, turned, smiled our way, and clutching her satchel full of papers, walked across and down the road two hundred feet to her apartment above the Bennett's farm house.

Uncle William waited for her to leave,

then walked over to our car. Looking at Dad,
he smiled. "What part do you think got
singed?" he grinned and raised his eyebrows in
question.

Dad glanced at me, then back to Uncle
Bill. "Makes a fellow wonder, doesn't it?" he
replied with a laugh. He got into the car and
started the engine as his brother snickered to
himself and walked over to the truck.

I wondered if we'd ever see the Model T
again.

As a consequence of lighting the teacher's
butt on fire, Jim and I had to walk to school
for the next two weeks. A couple of mornings
were quite cold and we were thankful when
sympathetic parents stopped to give us a ride.

The rest of the fall passed uneventfully
into winter. Getting to school was sometimes
a challenge, but we had fun and learned a lot
with the country kids. Christmas was

especially enjoyable. The students decorated the school house with handmade decorations and the entire student body put on a Christmas pageant for our families and the farm neighbors.

Chapter 8

After Christmas, winter settled in with a
vengeance. One Friday night Granddad got the
Model T stuck in the snow outside of town and
became so disgusted with it to the point that
he once more gave it to Jim and me. The next
morning we walked out with shovels and some
burlap bags for traction and dug for about an
hour to get the car out. It was cold when we

started, but both of us were sweating like farm hands in an August hay field by the time we were done shoveling and pushing on the old Tin Lizzie. How Granddad got that car so deeply into the snow bank, we could never figure out. He must have been drinking, again. Later, Dad and Uncle William dug around in the back of the service station and found some tire chains for the rear wheels. We could go anywhere in that thing now. We took great delight in taking the town girls out to see our country school. Jim always wanted to bring along Sally, the one he ended up marrying later. We even rigged up a toboggan to pull Archie behind the car, until our moms found out. They ordered us to stop before we killed the little guy.

In late spring, Jim and I found ourselves, as usual, out by the creek. The very creek the little kids had warned us to stay away from. There was something about the flowing water though that attracted us like a magnet.

The maples' buds had started to burst and the apple blossoms had begun to fade. The ground wasn't so cold and farmers were busy working the fields around us. A few in our area still used horses on their farms. I never tired of staring out the high windows of the school house, watching them plod down the fields, stopping to rest on the headlands, then finish the turn and head back. The farmer rode on a sulky plow while huge Belgians, hooked four abreast, plodded along. At recess I watched with Janet, the eleventh grader, while the team across the road from the school worked the land. We could hear the creak of the harness and the scraping, sliding noise of the plow as they moved along. The horses tossed their heads and blew out through their noses as they passed, and the farmer

waved once then returned his attention to
watching the furrow.

Jim was over in the side yard with some of
the younger boys watching a new Oliver tractor
pull a two furrow plow with an older Hart-Parr
trailing along another two bottoms. In two
days they were done with the whole field;
plowing and discing. They were planting corn
with a John Deere check planter when the
horses across the road finished their plowing.
After the tractors were done planting, they
went across the road and helped the horses get
the corn in there too. In the spring of
thirty-five, people still helped one another.
Now it was a contest among the students to see
who would be first to spot the corn coming up.
A few of the older farm boys had taken off
school to stay home and help with the planting
on their own farms.

On the day Jim and I were looking in the

creek, I had parked the Model T on the edge of the drive at the east side of the school, as I usually did. I'd driven it through the late winter and into spring. Granddad made no attempt to borrow it.

Jim and I looked across the creek to the corn fields. Nothing so far. We checked the fields to the east and the west. Still nothing. The farm kids seemed unconcerned, but we were beginning to think the corn wouldn't come up.

Suddenly Jim pointed in the water, "Look at that," he fairly shouted. "That's the biggest fish I've ever seen!"

I followed his excited gaze and saw what looked at first like a submerged hunk of wood on the creek bottom. Its tail thrashed and it moved slowly along against the current. Before I could say anything, Jim had kicked off his shoes and socks and, rolling up his pant legs, plunged into the shallow creek.

"It's getting away," he called. "Lend me a hand. Quick!"

At its deepest the creek was about a foot or so deep, and this was in the spring with high water. The fish made a break for freedom and swam right into the shallows where I was leaning over to trap it. Jim was too fast for it though. When the fish paused to dodge my hands, he quickly slipped his hands under it and through its gills.

"Aha!" he declared as he stepped triumphantly onto the grassy bank, the fish flopping mightily, trying to get away. "Looks like a sucker," Jim stated.

"I think you're right," I agreed. We'd speared suckers with our dads just below the dam where the river flowed on the edge of town. This fish looked just like them. "What are you going to do with it?" I asked.

"I hate to throw it back, it's so big," he responded. "I can't put it in the bathtub. Mom would have a fit. I know, I can put it in the Chapel's cow tank. It'll sure surprise everyone." He grinned broadly.

"What are you going to do with it *now*?" I countered.

"Hmm," he thought a moment. "Hold it for a minute, then follow me."

"This can't be good," I thought. But I held the fish while he slipped on his socks and shoes, and handing it back, followed him anyway.

Jim carried the fish around the corner of the school house. The other kids were busy playing on the swings or chasing each other in a game of tag. Teacher sat under a tree eating an apple and reading a book. Probably one of the many apples the brown-nosers brought her in their lunches each day.

I entered the school house first. No one was there. Jim brought the fish in. It still gave a flop every so often.

"Lift the lid to the crock," he commanded.

'Not the drinking water!' I hissed. My eyes grew wide.

"Yes, now hurry up. This thing's getting heavy."

I removed the crock lid and Jim eased the fish into the water. The thing was so big it had to curl itself around in the bottom. It settled in and I replaced the lid. Just in time, too. Out front, the teacher rang the recess bell, and the kids straggled in all hot and sweaty. Jim and I hustled to our desks in the back and tried to look busy.

Teacher brought the class to order and we picked up where we left off before lunch. It was during the little kids' geography lesson that the first kid got thirsty. Her recess

drink at the pump had worn off. Jim and I
watched as she picked up the cup and held it
under the spigot. Filling the cup, she took a
long drink. Jim and I looked at each other
and snickered. We had to put our books in
front of our faces to avoid the teacher's
glare.

This went on throughout the afternoon.
Different students would leave their seats for
a drink and Jim and I would bust into giggles
and snickers.

When school ended for the day, instead of
heading out the door as usual, Jim and I hung
around the room. Some kids cleaned the board
while others took the erasures outside to clap
them together.

"Something I can help you boys with?" the
teacher inquired. She must have known
something was up.

"We thought maybe we'd help out and dump

the water crock for the day," Jim said.

The teacher became even more suspicious. She looked at us for a long while, then turned and walked to the water crock. Lifting the lid, she peered down into it. It was at that moment the fish decided to shift position. Maybe he had a stiff back. The water suddenly exploded into the teacher's face. The fish thrashed again. More water slopped up over the edge of the crock as teacher drew back, still holding the lid in her hand. She glared at us. Placing the lid back on the drinking crock with a firm clatter that made me wonder why it didn't break, she walked to the phone. Removing the ear piece, she turned the crank for the operator.

"Have a seat boys," she spoke as she cranked the phone. Water dripped from her hair onto the front of her dress. We didn't dare laugh.

Within moments she had spoken to our
fathers down at the gas station and to the
school board members. We were ordered to
remain at our desks.

Once again, within minutes it seemed, our
fathers showed up. This time they came
together in Uncle William's Ford pickup. The
stools came out and Jim and I were ordered to
the front of the room to sit on them while our
fathers sat on desks in the front row.
Moments later several board members showed up
to join them.

The teacher once again relayed in detail
our transgressions. Playing in the creek was
the least of our worries. The men looked at
us incredulously when the teacher got to the
part about the water crock and the fish curled
in the bottom and the kids drinking from the
crock all afternoon. All the kids except, of
course, Jim and myself.

Our dads and the school board men stared at their shoes or at the hats they were fumbling in their hands. I expected to see a rope brought out at any minute, and I did a mental check of the maple trees out front for the one with a limb sturdy enough and high enough.

Dad looked at Uncle William and nodded. Uncle William began to speak.

"We're very sorry for what has happened ma'am," he began. It almost sounded like Dad and Uncle William were the culprits. "The boys will be dealt with at home, we can assure you."

I didn't like the sound of that last line. I snuck a look at Jim. He was busy studying his finger nails.

"Anything you boys would like to say?" Dad finished up the discussion.

"I'm sorry," I tried to sound as

remorseful as I felt. I hoped it came across.

"Me too," Jim added. "I just couldn't let a prize fish like that go. It's a beauty. I wanted to take it home and then put it in someone's cow tank. It's too big for the bath-tub."

I could have sworn I heard one of the board members choke on a snicker.

"It's going back in the creek where it belongs," Uncle William said. And with that he stepped over, removed the crock lid and plunged his hand in to grasp the fish. He pulled it out, dripping and flapping, his fingers through its gills.

"Jeez," a board member said. Another gave a low whistle. Even with Uncle William holding the fish, it looked huge. It must have grown six inches during the afternoon!

Uncle William held the fish higher. I saw the look of admiration on the board members' faces and the look of disgust on the teacher's. I knew who the sportsmen were. I hoped it would earn us a little sympathy.

Dad cleared his throat. "That's some fish alright," he finally said. "Almost a shame to throw it back." Then he caught himself as the teacher threw a stormy glance his way. "Back it goes," he said. "And you boys owe the teacher an apology."

Uncle William was heading out the door with the fish. Two school board members went with him. "Wish I'd brought my Kodak," one of them remarked.

"Teacher," Jim began. "You're right to be upset with us. We weren't thinking. I guess I was overcome with the thought of getting that trophy home in one piece, and didn't think through the consequences."

Teacher was real big on thinking through consequences.

"Same goes for me," I spoke up in what I hoped was a clear voice.

"Well, boys. Seeing as how you two have been so good all winter and this spring, apology accepted." and she smiled that winning smile at us.

I knew she was thinking about the outhouse incident.

A weight seemed to be lifted from the room. Dad and the remaining board members brightened up considerably. They shook hands with the teacher and with each other and Dad led me out the door.

He held out his hand and I didn't even have to ask what he wanted. I pulled the key to the Model T from my pocket and handed it over.

"Get in," he said. I climbed into the passenger side. Jim was climbing into the Ford pickup. His father returned from the sucker rescue mission and slid behind the wheel. Our dads bid "Goodbye" to the board members and the teacher and we were off.

"Granddad said he needs to borrow the T tomorrow," Dad said as we rattled along the dirt road toward town. "Said he has some errands to run." Then after a pause, "I think it might be best to let him borrow it."

"Sure," I replied. What else could I say. I wasn't in a position to bargain.

For our "prank" Jim and I had to stay after school and wipe down the chalk board, sweep the floor, empty the trash, and perform other general janitorial duties for the rest of the school year. After the first couple of days we actually didn't mind. The teacher really was a nice sort after all. We got along just great and we worked hard to regain her trust. We never were allowed to touch the water crock though.

Chapter 9

The next day, after borrowing the old
Model T, Granddad traded it in on a used
Studebaker. The Ford Garage seemed to have a
lot of used Studebakers on their car lot. At
that time my father was driving a 1929
Studebaker Commander. A nice car back then
and now-a-days too. When I was nineteen I
bought my first real car. It was the
dentist's '34 Chevy that he had bought new.

It had a rumble seat. Man,... that car was the berries!"

The old man paused and looked at his watch. "Jeez, I've got to get running," he said. "It's been nice chatting with you boys."

I told him to drop by anytime, and I meant it. Frank nodded and smiled in agreement. The old man wasn't the same little old man who had walked through the doorway. Somehow, in him I could see some of the small town boy that lived a childhood just like a million other small town boys. He had shared a part of himself. From listening to his story, I went back in time to my own youth. Back to fishing on the mill pond and camping with my brothers.

Every July Fourth we'd go up to the school grounds to ride the rides and eat hot dogs, candy cotton, and popcorn until we were ready to burst. I almost wished the old man and I were the same age so we could have shared our childhoods together. It sounded as though he had as much fun as I had. Even though I wasn't there to experience the summers of his youth, I felt fortunate to have him share his memories with me.

We walked with him out to his car and saw him off down the road. The sun was low in the west. It was quitting time. Without talking, Frank and I began to roll the tractor tires from the front of the store into the open service bays. Frank stopped just inside the large overhead door and leaned into the tread of the giant tire he was rolling. "You know", he said, "Those retired guys sure do talk a lot."

I leaned my tire against the stack. "Yea," I agreed. And grabbing the rope attached to the overhead door, pulled it shut.

John Riley lives with his wife, Susan, on a small farm near Parma, in rural southern Michigan. Besides farming, he is also an elementary school teacher, having switched to teaching from a nearly twenty year career in the computer field.

John has been writing poetry and short stories for most of his adult life. The Model T Connection is his first published novel. He and

Susan raised three children; one boy, and two girls.

Besides farming and writing, John enjoys tinkering with his classic

Cockshutt-Co-ops and Moline tractors. During fair weather his daily

driver is a 1964 Studebaker.